Action Rhymes

Twinkle, Twinkle, Little Star

and

Spaceship, Spaceship, Zooming High

Notes for adults

TADPOLES ACTION RHYMES provide support for newly independent readers and can also be used by adults for sharing with young children.

The language of action rhymes is often already familiar to an emergent reader and gives a highly supportive early reading experience.

The alternative rhymes extend this reading experience further, and encourage children to play with language and try out their own rhymes and actions.

If you are reading this book with a child, here are a few suggestions:

1. Make reading fun! Choose a time to read when you and the child are relaxed and have time to share the story.

2. Recite the rhyme together before you start reading. What might the alternative rhyme be about? Why might the child like it?

3. Encourage the child to reread the rhyme and do the actions, and to retell it in their own words, using the illustrations to remind them what has happened.

4. Point out together the rhyming words when the whole rhymes are repeated on pages 12 and 22 (developing phonological awareness will help with decoding) and encourage the child to make up their own new rhymes.

5. Give praise! Remember that small mistakes need not always be corrected.

First published in 2010 by
Franklin Watts
338 Euston Road
London NW1 3BH

Franklin Watts Australia
Level 17/207 Kent Street
Sydney NSW 2000

Spaceship, Spaceship Zooming High
© Wes Magee 2010
Illustration © Mike Byrne 2010

The rights of Wes Magee to be identified as the author of Spaceship, Spaceship Zooming High and Mike Byrne as the illustrator of this Work have been asserted in accordance with the Copyright, Designs and Patents Act, 1988.

ISBN 978 0 7496 9368 8 (hbk)
ISBN 978 0 7496 9374 9 (pbk)

Series Editor: Melanie Palmer
Series Advisors: Dr Hilary Minns and Catherine Glavina
Series Designer: Peter Scoulding

Printed in China

Franklin Watts is a division of Hachette Children's Books an Hachette Livre UK company.
www.hachettelivre.co.uk

Twinkle, Twinkle, Little Star

Retold by Wes Magee
Illustrated by Mike Byrne

W
FRANKLIN WATTS
LONDON • SYDNEY

Mike Byrne

"I have always enjoyed drawing my own stories and pictures about space and far away galaxies. There are so many adventures you can have!"

Twinkle, twinkle, little star,

how I wonder what
you are.

Up above the world
so high,

8

like a diamond
in the sky.

Twinkle, twinkle, little star,

how I wonder what you are.

Twinkle, Twinkle, Little Star

 Twinkle, twinkle, little star,

how I wonder what you are.

Up above the world so high,

like a diamond in the sky.

Twinkle, twinkle, little star,

how I wonder what you are.

 Can you point to the rhyming words?

Spaceship, Spaceship, Zooming High

by Wes Magee
Illustrated by Mike Byrne

Wes Magee

"I spot something different each time I look up at the night sky. I've only seen one spaceship so far. What can you see?

Spaceship, spaceship, zooming high,

far across the
starry sky.

Past the Moon
and over Mars,

18

racing past the
shooting stars.

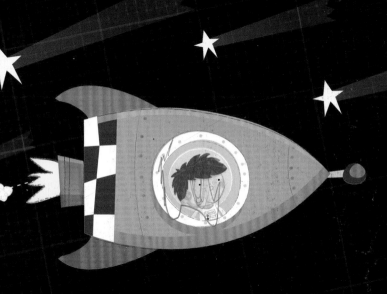

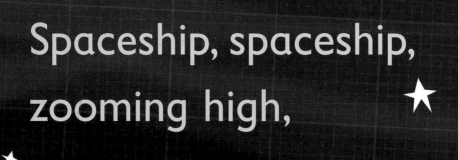

Spaceship, spaceship,
zooming high,

far across the
starry sky.

Spaceship, Spaceship, Zooming High

Spaceship, spaceship,

zooming high,

far across the starry sky.

Past the Moon and over Mars,

racing past the shooting stars.

Spaceship, spaceship,

zooming high,

far across the starry sky.

Can you point to the
rhyming words?

Puzzle Time!

How many spaceships can you see in this picture?

Answers

There are 5 spaceships
in the picture.